Shifty McGifty
AND
SLIPPERY SAM

PIRATES AHOY!

First published 2022 by Nosy Crow Ltd
The Crow's Nest, 14 Baden Place,
Crosby Row, London, SE1 1YW, UK

Nosy Crow Eireann Ltd
44 Orchard Grove, Kenmare,
Co Kerry, V93 FY22, Ireland

www.nosycrow.com

ISBN 978 1 83994 581 6 (HB)
ISBN 978 1 83994 582 3 (PB)

Nosy Crow and associated logos are trademarks and/or
registered trademarks of Nosy Crow Ltd.

Text © Tracey Corderoy 2022
Illustrations © Steven Lenton 2022

The right of Tracey Corderoy to be identified as the author of this work and of
Steven Lenton to be identified as the illustrator of this work has been asserted.
All rights reserved.

A CIP catalogue record for this book is available from the British Library.

Printed in Italy

Papers used by Nosy Crow are made from
wood grown in sustainable forests.

10 9 8 7 6 5 4 3 2 1 (HB)
10 9 8 7 6 5 4 3 2 1 (PB)

For Wilfred Alan Owen
(and his very lovely granny!).
Much love to you both . . .
T.C.

For Big-Eared Bob, who kept
me smiling during lockdown
(you can spot him throughout
this book, ooh arr!).
S.L.

Shifty McGifty

AND SLIPPERY SAM

PIRATES AHOY!

Tracey Corderoy

Illustrated by
Steven Lenton

nosy
crow

One bright, breezy morning, as fine as could be,
two swashbuckling dogs bravely rowed out to sea.
They used to be robbers, then found they could bake,
so gave up on crime for a job filled with cake!

But though Sam and Shifty had baked near and far . . .

. . . they'd never made cupcakes for
pirates, ooh arr!

"Yo-ho! Are you ready to party?" called Sam.
"Why, yes," Captain Chucklebeard chuckled. "I am!
We dug up some **treasure**, you see – quite a lot!
So, 'treat time' I said to my crew. And why not!"

The old galley kitchen was cosy and warm,
as Shifty and Sam quickly baked up a storm.
Their cookies were crunchy. Their pastries were light.
And as for their octo-cake – wow – what a sight!

But then, as the band for the
party trooped through . . .

"My buns!" Shifty frowned.
"There were three –
now there's two?"

Sam saw the lead singer had
quickened his pace.
And could that be **icing**
he spied on his face?

The party kicked off and the dancing was wild.
"We love a good bop," Captain Chucklebeard smiled.

"And look at our treasure! It shines like the moon."
The band were so dazed they went quite out of tune!

Some party games followed, all noisy and daft.
"Oh look! Pin-the-tail-on-the-parrot!" Sam laughed.
But poor Captain Chucklebeard, try as he might,
kept getting it wrong, to his crew's great delight!

"Psst – Sam," Shifty whispered. "It's time for . . . you know."
"Our octo-cake!" Sam gave a nod. "Right – let's go."

But outside the kitchen, they let out a cry.
"The treasure chest's vanished!" gasped Shifty.
"Oh my!"

And just as the band shuffled out
of the door –

ker-chink!

– something golden dropped
onto the floor.

"They've got it!" cried Sam.
"But I don't understand.
Why take it? Unless . . .
they're not really a band!"

The boys quickly followed, and up on the deck . . .
"They're pirates! But bad ones," gulped Shifty. "Oh, heck!"

"Just bad?" Captain Sharpwhiskers
called with a scowl.
"We're much worse than bad.
Why, by jiggers, we're foul!"

Their rock-band disguises flew into the sky,
as Sharpwhiskers shouted a jeering, "Goodbye!"

"Their **ship!**" shouted Sam, as it loomed into view.
"Oh no! They'll **escape** – with the treasure chest too!"

The baddies sailed off.

"No, you don't!" Shifty said.
"We'll get back that treasure.
Quick! Full speed ahead!"

They pulled up the anchor and shouted, "Let's go!" . . .

. . . but Chucklebeard's ship was too leaky and slow.

"They've won," said the captain.
He heaved a big sigh, when . . .

"Squawk!" went his parrot,
high up in the sky.

She fluttered her feathers then zoomed like a rocket
and pecked something stringy from Sam's apron pocket.
The something was liquorice. Super strong too.

"Oh wait!" Shifty cried. "Polly knows what to do!"
They watched as she flew to the bad pirates' mast . . .

. . . and wrapped round the liquorice,
tying it fast.

"A zipwire!" grinned Shifty.
"Jump on, Sam – what fun!
The octo-cake too, please."
It had to be done.

Then over they went, yelling . . .

. . . "Robbers – take that!"

And down came the cake
with a whopping great . . .

SPLAT!

The crew couldn't steer –
they were **iced**, head to boot . . .

. . . so Shifty and Sam quickly
snatched back the loot.

And just as the ship – with a jolly big bump –
crashed into an island, the boys bellowed,

"Jump!"

A soggy swim later, the gold back in place,
old Chucklebeard had **such** a smile on his face.
"You rescued the treasure!" he chuckled.
"Hooray!"

The boys – and his parrot –
had just saved the day.

The pirates sailed home. What a sight met their eyes!
"I bought a new ship," said the captain. "Surprise!
The gold was for **this**," he explained with a grin.
The crew gave a cheer and they all piled right in.

Then Shifty and Sam put
their feet up and . . .

. . . WOW!

Nothing – but **nothing** – could spoil their day now!